PASHUL

MOHAMMADREZA GHAFOURI

Title: PASHUL

Author: Mohammadreza Ghafouri

Translator: Zohreh Parvaz

Illustrator: Elham Saheb Jamei, Tina Tajalifar

Layout: Raed Parvaz

ISBN: 978-1942912514

Publisher: Supreme Art, USA

Once upon a time, Arman and his mother Arezoo were driving back home from school. It was autumn, and the yellow leaves of soft trees fell slowly on the ground, rushing across the street without looking at the sides, a kitten hit a car and was thrown forward, Arezoo at once got out of the car and picked the kitten, then rushed her to the vet. After examining it, the doctor found that the leg was broken and kindly fixed its leg. Arman and his mother thanked the doctor for helping the kitten and took her to their house, they brought her some milk. The little cat was so hungry that it rushed to the milk bowel and licked the milk inside it to the end. While feeding the kitten, Arezoo had made her decision to take care it until it recovered and was fine again. Arezoo looked into Arman's eyes and realized that he has agreed with her, so they decided to keep the kitten until its leg was fine again and because it was a female cat, they named it Pashul.

VETERINARY

It was autumn, Pashul sat for hours under the shade of trees in the garden and watched the branches shaken by the wind. The fall of the leaves seemed interesting to her. One of these autumn days, a crow on the branch of one of these trees was watching Arezoo feeding Pashul and showing love to her. The crow said to herself, "I wish I was Pashul, and Arezoo gave her love to me."While Pashul was watching the birds flying, she was listening to their beautiful song. She was watching the chickens, roosters, ducks, sparrows, and crows in the garden, and wished to be their friends and play with them, but they did not like her. Pashul also watched the colorful fish in the pool. Dancing of the fish in the water was something new to her. Arezoo had already told Pashul not to get close to the pool, because she couldn't swim and could drown in it.

Days passed, Arezoo and Arman liked Pashul more than before. Pashul also displayed her love and friendship by loosening herself to them. Pashul's leg was getting better slowly, and she was learning more day after day. When her leg was fine again, Arezoo took Pashul to the street to show her that she coul cross the pedestrian when she saw the green light and to take the overpass, if it was available. He also taught Pashul to always pay attention to the instructions of the police to avoid any problems.

Arezoo taught the names of birds to Pashul, and she knew the rooster, canary, sparrows and the crow. She did not like the sound of the crow, because their loud noise disturbed her while asleep early in the morning. Arezoo and Arman took Pashul to the horse track. They had a horse called Mahpishoni (the Moon's Forehead); Pashul soon became friend with Mahpishoni, and even took a ride on it with Arezoo. It was very enjoyable for her to take a ride on horseback and look around the landscape.

After a few days, Arezoo and Arman had taken Pashul to the Garden of Birds with them to see the birds and get familiar with them. The garden of the birds was very beautiful and big. The song of birds was heard all over the garden. Pashul saw the ostrich, the world's largest bird, but it could not fly. The ostrich was very fast and was the best runner; it was even bigger than Mahpishoni. In the garden of birds Pashul liked the eagle, but the eagle looked at Arezoo and Pashul with a special pride.

Arezoo told Pashul about the migratory birds. She said, the birds migrated from north to south in winter, because in the winter, south was warmer than north, thus the birds could spend the hard and cold winter of the north in the south.

Pashul decided to go to the Persian Gulf to see the migratory birds there. Pashul took permission from Arezoo and Arman for this journey, and took the train. It was very interesting to travel on the train. After passing by the cities, villages and deserts, she finally reached the Persian Gulf. Pashul had promised Arezoo to be careful of all motorized and non-motorized vehicles such as bicycles.

Pashul arrived in the Persian Gulf at the port city of Bandar Abbas, where it was water as much as she could see. It was much bigger than the pool in Arezoo's house, how calm, blue and beautiful it was, with a variety of passenger and cargo vessels and boats. He loved the hot sand and shells on the beach very much. She collected some shells from the beach. She liked to give them as a gift to Arman. Lying down on the sand on a Persian Gulf beach, she saw a cat wearing a beautiful necklace, the name of the cat was Meouraja. She made friends with Meouraja. Meouraja was a tomcat and a traveler that had come to Iran from India to see the whales and dolphins of the Indian Ocean and the sharks of the Persian Gulf, because this cat belonged to Ramarjah, he was called Meouraja. Pashul explained to Meouraja how she had traveled to the Persian Gulf to see the migratory birds.

Meouraja showed Pashul all the migratory birds flying and swimming in the Persian Gulf. How beautiful and lovely those birds were. Pashul greeted them loudly. Meouraja told Pashul about the parrots and peacocks of India. Parrots that were the most beautiful in the world and invited Pashul to travel with him to India. Pashul, who liked the kindness and behavior of Meouraja decided to join him in the travel. Pashul asked Meouraja where his necklace came from? Meouraja said, it was a pearl necklace that was donated to him by Nila, a necklace made of pearls and oyster shell which was expensive.

A few hours later, Meouraja, along with Pashul, boarded the ship to travel to India. The ship was floating and blowing horn on the water, and then began to move. While the ship was crossing in the Persian Gulf, Meouraja showed the sharks to Pashul. They were very large. After a while, it was night and the stars and the moon had appeared with a special sparkle. Meouraja and Pashul went to the cabin after a long and beautiful day to rest.

The next day came. They were approaching the Indian Ocean. Meouraja told

Pashul to go on the deck to watch the whales and dolphins. Meouraja talked to

the sailor on the deck that showed him the whales, and said that the ship was

going towards the whales, so they could easily watch them. At this time, the

dolphins were diving around the ship. The chef of Peter's ship became friend with

Pashul and Meouraja, and served them delicious foods.

A few days passed, after a long and far-reaching trip, they finally arrived at the port city of Mumbai. Meouraja took Pashul to the city and the people there warmly welcomed her. They also shared their own foods with her. Meouraja took Pashul to visit historical monuments such as Khosro Garden, Flora Statue and Taj Mahal Grand Hotel. Then he took Pashul to the Ramaraja's Palace, where Ramaraja, along with his wife, Nila and her daughter Aditi, were very pleased to see Meouraja and his friend Pashul, and warmly welcomed them. Nila and Aditi were very happy to see Pashul and smiled at her.

The next morning, Meouraja and Aditi showed various parts of the palace and garden to Pashul. At the corner of the castle, an iron bird was resting. It was Ramaraja's personal plane. The plane was even larger than an ostrich. Aditi and Meouraja said to Pashul that the plane flew like birds. Aditi and Nila became friends with Pashul. Nila made delicious food for Pashul. Pashul became very intimate with them and told the story of her friendship with Arezoo and Arman.

After a few days in the palace, they left it for the jungle. At a corner in the jungle, an elephant and amahout were waiting to pick the tourists and passengers to the jungle. Meouraja talked to the mahout, and told him his destination, and then the elephant picked Meouraja and Pashul with his trunk and put them on his back. This elephant was much larger than Mahpishoni. As they were riding toward the jungle, they were talking with the elephant, and told him their names and became friends with him. Meouraja told the elephant how he became friend with Pashul, and how he traveled from Iran to India to see the peacocks and parrots. The elephant said his name was Chandah. Also the mahout was happy for his trip with Meouraja and Pashul, and told them that he had never brought a cat to the woods before. The mahout said his name was Adhara, which means God's closest friend.

Pashul and Meouraja, on the elephant back got close to the branches of trees.

Adhara told them to be careful with them, as these branches might hurt them.

Along the way, they reached the entrance to the jungle, writing in front of it:

"Please do not throw waste and respect the nature and the jungle, and let us be

kind to the nature." The sound of all birds and animals was heard in the woods.

Adhara showed a nearby tiger to Pashul and Meouraja, the tiger looked very

much like the cats, but it was larger than them, Pashul greeted the tiger. They

continued their journey after having known the tiger.

Let's Be Kind To The
Nature

After covering a distance, they reached the parrots. Meouraja showed the parrots

of the jungle that were sitting on the branches of trees. Then Adhara talked to the

parrots and told them that Pashul had come a long way from Iran to see them

there. The parrots welcomed Pashul and Meouraja. The scene was very beautiful;

all the parrots were colorful and different from those in the garden of birds, which

Pashul had seen before. Having made friend with Pashul, the jungle parrots told

her to say hello to the parrots of Iran.

After a while, the elephant put down Pashul and Meouraja by his trunk, so that they could walk in the beautiful jungle. The mahout, Adhara told them not to go too far, they might get lost. After walking a distance in the middle of the jungle, heard a troubled voice. They moved forward and found a beautiful bird had its feet stuck in the roots of a tree, so they rushed to save it. Pashul said that this beautiful bird should be the same peacock in India, so she was very happy to see the beautiful peacock of India closely and to have helped her. The peacock introduced herself to them as Brinda. Pashul and Meouraja also introduced themselves to the peacock.

Meouraja told the peacock that Pashul had come all the way from Iran to see the

Indian Peacocks in the jungle and India. Then Brinda took them to a part of the

jungle where all the peacocks were gathered to make them familiar with their

friends. All the peacocks had gathered there, Brinda told his friends how Pashul

and Meouraja had saved her life, so some of the peacocks thanked them for

saving Brinda's life by opening all their feathers to them. Pashul was surprised to

see the beautiful feathers of the peacocks. The peacocks started singing to thank

Pashul and Meouraja. Some butterflies also danced with the singing of the

peacocks.

One of the peacocks gave two of its feathers to Pashul and Meouraja as gratitude and friendship. This was the first and most beautiful gift that Pashul had taken in her life. Pashul was very happy and said to herself that she would show the feather to all the birds of the garden and tell them that the peacocks of India were friends with them and would give it as a gift to Arezoo. Pashul then put feather in her backpack. At this time, all the monkeys who witnessed the incident clapped for Pashul and Meouraja on the tree and laid a necklace of flowers around their necks, a necklace that was much more beautiful than the pearl necklace of Meouraja. Pashul thanked all the peacocks and monkeys, and wished Arezoo was there to give her the necklace as a gift, because she looked more beautiful with that necklace.

Then Pashul and Meouraja said goodbye to the peacocks and the monkeys, and returned to Adhara and Chanda to get back to the city. When they came out of the jungle, they said goodbye to Adhara and Chanda. When they arrived at the palace, it was almost early in the evening. Meouraja told Ramaraja, Nila and Aditi what happened today in the jungle for Pashul and him, and gave the peacock feather as a gift to Aditi. At this time everyone clapped for Pashul and Meouraja. After a while, Ramaraja said that tomorrow he would go to Rajasthan State and the city of Bikaner on his airplane for business. He told Pashul and Meouraja that there is a beautiful temple there that all its inhabitants are rats, and if they like, they can come along with Nila and Aditi for this journey with him.

The next morning everyone was on the plane. Ramaraja himself was the pilot.

How beautiful it was to see the jungle and rivers from the sky. The plane was

flying higher than all the birds Pashul had seen all her life. Pashul then realized

how enjoyable the flight was. After a few hours they reached the city of Bikaner,

and landed at the airport, where there were even larger airplanes there.

Ramaraja showed the way to the village of Deshnok and told them to be around

the plane tomorrow afternoon to return to Mumbai. Then they said goodbye to

each other.

At this time, on the way to the temple, Pashul and Meouraja came to a spring of water, surrounded by beautiful and green trees. Pashul told Meouraja that it was hot and she had to drink some water, then they went to the fountain and drank from the cool water of the fountain. Inside the fountain of water, sitting on a rock, a frog was singing; at that time, an owl was watching Pashul and Meouraja from above a tree near the spring, and then asked their names, they greeted the owl, the eyes of the owl shone and they told him their names. The owl also said his name to Pashul and Meouraja; His name was Bakul and he was glad to meet them. Then the owl asked them: "Where are you going in this night?" "We are going to the beautiful temple of Rats, answered Meouraja, later a beautiful fox appeared from behind the green bushes, and his name was Shania. The fox said hello to Pashul and Meouraja, and welcomed them. Shania had shiny eyes, more beautiful than Bakul's, and her tail looked like a beautiful pillow. Shania told Pashul and Meouraja: "Drink from our water."

Bakul asked Pashul and Meouraja why they wanted to go to the Temple of Rats?

Meouraja replied:"Pashul has come from Iran, the beautiful Persian Gulf and the beautiful land of Persia there and I intend to show her the beautiful Temple of the Rats." Shania, who had already been to the temple, said, the Temple of Rats is like a stronghold, with its treasury of precious gold and jewels, jewels that are not found anywhere in the world and it is protected by powerful soldiers. Shania told Meouraja and Pashul that there was a long way to the temple, but I know a man named Adad, who fed me and Bakul every night. He is a very kind man who passes by here every night and takes fresh grass for his cattle. His house passes through the way to the temple, and I ask him to accompany you to that place.

At that moment, a car appeared from far away with its head lights on. Bakul said to Shania: The kind man has brought us food." Then he said to Pashul: "I would like to go to the temple with you, but they won't let me in, because flying over the temple is forbidden, but I will wait for you here tomorrow night when you return from the temple, to tell me about its beauties." Adad came there and got off his car and said hello to Shania and gave them some food. Bakul introduced his new friends to Adad from over the tree and told him that Pashul had come a long way from Iran and the Persian Gulf to see the beauties of India. He said: "They want to go to the beautiful Temple of Rats and ask Adad to accompany Pashul and Meouraja to the temple." Pashul and Meouraja also said hello to Adad and thanked him.

Adad said to Pashul and Meouraja; "I will take you to the beautiful Temple of the Rats", then Pashul and Meouraja got into his car and lay down on the soft straw, staring at the stars and the moon. Pashul said to Meouraja: "Star in the Indian sky look more beautiful and more brilliant than all the stars in the sky of our city. Meouraja said, the stars in the deserts of Iran are most beautiful in the world. They continued their way until they finally arrived at the Temple of the Rats and got off the car. Adad said, take care of yourselves.

Covering a distance, they reached a great temple in the heart of the desert. The night appeared, and all the desert stars were illuminating. When Pashul and Meouraja entered the temple, suddenly hundreds of rats attacked them and tied them with ropes to the pillars. At this time, a white rat, with a crown on his head entered the temple, he was the King of the Rats, and told them cats are not allowed into the temple of Rats, and they should be punished for that.

At this time, the minister saw the peacock feather in Pashul's backpack, and asked her, "What is that feather doing in your backpack?"

In response to this question, Meouraja told the story of saving the peacock in the jungle and their friendship with the peacocks for the king and the minister. The King of Rats was thinking of something, and then told Meouraja and Pashul: "If you were good friends for the peacocks then you could be good friends for us too". When the king said that, all the rats shouted hurrah, so the king said, "Meouraja and Pashul are our guests and free them". The King ordered the Minister to celebrate tonight for Pashul and Meouraja and serve them with cake and milk.

At dinner time, the king asked Pashul: "For what did you come from abroad to India? Is it tourism?" In reply to the King, Pashul told the story of her accident with Arezoo, and how she was saved by her, as well as the kindness and beauties of Arezoo. The King and the Queen said to Pashul to give their greetings to Arezoo. Pashul told more about Arezoo, and how she taught her to cross the street, and how she took her to the horse track to give her a ride on her horseback Mahpishoni, and then took her to the garden of birds.

Pashul then told the adventure of seeing migratory birds and her friendship with Meouraja for the king and said that Meouraja had come to the Persian Gulf to see the whales, dolphins and sharks, where she met him and they decided to travel together to see the peacocks and parrots of India closely. After talking to Pashul, the King asked Meouraja about his life; Meouraja said that he lived with Ramaraja, Nila and Aditi, and then he told the King about Ramaraja, that he is a businessman who favors him a lot. His wife, Nila is also very kind and makes tasty foods for him. Then he said that Ramaraja is a pilot. He brought Pashul and him in his own aircraft to the city of Bikaner to see this beautiful temple.

At that time, all the Rats, which numbered twenty thousand, shouted hurrah for

Arezoo, Ramaraja, Nila, Meouraja and Pashul. The King turned to the Rats and

told them: "We should listen to Arezoo and do what she said while crossing the

street."He also said to Pashul and Meouraja:"You gave us a great lesson". At that

time, the King called the treasurer in a loud voice and ordered him to take Pashul

and Meouraja to the treasury of the temple and give them two gold necklaces of

the Temple of Karni Mata to be dedicated to Arezoo and Nila for appreciation.

The Queen of the Rats said: "With these necklaces, all rats everywhere in the

world will become friend with Arezoo and Nila, and will not hesitate to help

them."

When they entered the treasury, a light sparked in the eyes of Pashul. The treasurer then donated two pieces of gold necklaces to Pashul and Meouraja. Pashul thought to herself that the beauty of Arezoo will double with this necklace, she thought Arezoo had saved her life, in return for her favor, this necklace isn't too worthy."

On that night, the Rats, together with Pashul and Meouraja, were celebrating and dancing till morning, the King and Queen of the Rats were happy to have such guests. The Queen liked to learn more about Iran, so she urged Pashul to talk about Iran and its people. Pashul said, people of Iran are very kind. And the city of Isfahan has nothing less than the beauty of Mumbai. The next morning, Meouraja said to the King and Queen that they should return to the airport because Ramaraja was waiting for them there, and they want to go back to Mumbai with him. Meouraja said to the King of Rats: "Shania and Bakul are two of our friends who live by the spring near the temple, they would like to come here and see your temple, but they cannot". The King told Meouraja that tomorrow he would send a messenger to invite them to visit the temple for dinner".

The King ordered some of the rats to escort Pashul and Meouraja to the airport, so that they could arrive earlier and not to get tired. Pashul and Meouraja said farewell to the King, the Queen and all the rats, and then took the underground way. This beautiful spiral tunnel was so long that no other cat had entered before. The wonderfully beautiful architecture of the tunnel astonished Pashul and Meouraja. After passing through several tunnels, they finally arrived at the airport where Aditi, Ramarjah and Nila were waiting for them. Then they got on the plane with their friends and headed for Mumbai.

During the flight on the plane, Meouraja explained with great enthusiasm all the events of the temple, and the warm reception by the King and Queen of the Rats for Aditi, Ramaraja, and Nila, and delivered the King and Queen's greetings to them. He also gave Nila the King's gift, the gold necklace. Nila was very happy when she saw that beautiful gold necklace, and appreciated. Meouraja said that Pashul has also received the same necklace from the King of Rats, which she intends to give to Arezoo as a gift.

The next day, Pashul's eyes dropped into the great dome of Ramaraja's Palace, the height of the temple tempted her to climb it up and from there to the top of the dome to watch the beautiful surrounding landscape of the palace. The wind blew and the dancing of trees and singing of the birds was one of the most beautiful moments she had ever seen. Pashul was busy in her mind, and was desperate for the city of Isfahan and was dreaming to see it again. Tears were gathering in her eyes, so she said to her friends that they must go back to Iran and to Arezoo. Aditi suggested that Pashul stayed there and live with them, but she was thinking about Arezoo and Iran. Pashul thought, how she could forget all the kindness of Arezoo, so she did not accept Aditi's offer. Pashul invited his friends to travel to Iran to visit Arezoo and Arman to see all beauties of that country. Then she said, "I am waiting for you to come to Iran to see that beautiful lovely land." Nila said: "I will travel to Iran at the earliest opportunity." They all accompanied Pashul to the port of Mumbai. Pashul said farewell to her friends and boarded the ship. The ship whistled, and quietly left the port for Iran. It was very hard for Pashul to forget the friendly and kind people of India, but thinking about going back to Iran made her glad. Nila told Pashul to give her greetings to Arezoo and waved her hand for Pashul.

On her way at the sea, Pashul was thinking about the kind people of India, who were all smiling. She had lost her heart for them. When she reached the Indian Ocean, she remembered the names of the whales and the dolphins, and said hello to all of them. When she arrived in the Persian Gulf, she greeted the sharks. After a while, Pashul had arrived in the beautiful port city of Bandar Abbas and got on a train. After passing through various cities and deserts, she finally arrived in the beautiful city of Isfahan, and then she headed for Arezoo's house.

She first saw the crow, which was very happy to see her, the crow said hello to Pashul and told her that he had missed her greatly, and Arezoo was so concerned about her. Then the crow cried out loudly to tell other crows about her arrival. Other crows joined him to get to Arezoo's house. Arezoo was so surprised to see the crows and asked them: "What news have you brought me?" One of them said, "Good news Drs. Arezoo Pashul has come.", then all the crows said: Pashul has come, Welcome Pashul!" For the good news of Pashul's arrival, Arezoo gave the crows a basket full of walnuts as reward, each crow took one. After a while, Pashul entered the garden and ran happily to Arezoo and Arman and said hello to them. Pashul showed her love and affection by wagging her tail and jumping to the embrace of Arezoo. Holding her in a hug, Arezoo began to pat her head. Arezoo and Arman were so excited to see Pashul again.

She brought out the beautiful peacock feather from her backpack and showed it

to other birds, and then she gave it to Arezoo, and put necklaces of the Temple of

Karni Mata around her neck. Arezoo looked more beautiful with the necklace, and

remembered The King and Queen of Rats of the temple Karni Mata to her. Then

she gave the shells she had brought from the Persian Gulf to Arman as a gift.

Pashul had a lot of tales from this long journey. She wanted to tell Arezoo, Arman,

Mahpishoni, and her other friends all the adventures of this long journey.

50 days later

Hello cats, I've come to the right place here. Isfahan is a big and beautiful city. The bridge of thirty-three is a masterpiece of architecture. I never saw snow in the city Of Mumbai, it never snows there. Where's Pashul and Arezoo's house? What a cute cat! What a pretty necklace she is wearing! Are you a friend of Arezoo, or Pashul?

Friends of Pashul are our friends too. Pashul is a good friend who shares her food with us. You take this street up to the crossroads, be careful of cars and motorbikes. Walk through the pedestrian crossing to the other side of the street. Go into the first alley, with a large jungle tree. It has a large pool full of colorful fish; it is the house of Arezoo, Arman and Pashul. Do not get close to the pool, because you can't swim, and you might be drowned.

Say hello to beautiful Arezoo and Pashul.

Mom, I think, it sounds like a hungry cat out there. Arezoo told her son Arman to give the cat a little of the rice-milk in the refrigerator. The cat greeted Arman, and said: "I am Meouraja, Pashul's friend, and you must be Arman. Glad to meet you. I hope I've not disturbed you." Arman welcomed Meouraja with pleasure. Then he called his mother. Mom! Mom! Meouraja Pashul's friend has come here! I knew that Meouraja finally would travel to Iran. The rats let me know month earlier that Meouraja had decided to come to Iran. Meouraja greeted Arezoo, when he saw her, and Arezoo warmly welcomed him. Meouraja said: "I have come to Iran to visit Arman, Arman and Pashul. Arezoo put a bowl of rice-milk in front of Meouraja, who was very hungry. Meouraja said that Pashul soon goes to sleep inside her tree house in the garden after eating her dinner. He loved the good taste of the rice-milk made by Arezoo, and thanked her for the dinner.

Arman, who was looking at Meouraja, told her mother: "How polite this cat is, and what a beautiful necklace he is wearing!"Meouraja said, "Nila gave me this beautiful and expensive pearl necklace as a gift, it is so valuable to me, whenever I miss her in a travel and feel for Nila, this necklace gives me hope, as well as the nights I am away from her, so I look at the polar star to see her there". Arezoo embraced Meouraja and took him to Pashul on the terrace of the tree house and told him, go to bed in the tree house; there is room for both of you inside there.

Pashul was awakened by their noise, and asked: "Is it morning or have the rats brought us news? "Arezoo said: "Meouraja, your friend from India has come here."Pashul was so glad to see Meouraja and greeted him. Meouraja told Pashul: "I have come to Iran forever, and I would love to stay here. "Pashul watched Arezoo and said, "Can Meouraja stay with us?" Arezoo kindly answered that Meouraja can live with us as long as he liked. Meouraja said: "Thank you for your favor, you kind and beautiful Arezoo." Then he went with Pashul into the tree house. Also, Arezoo told Arman that it was late and he had to brush his teeth and go to bed to wake up tomorrow morning, and not be late at school.

Early in the morning, they all woke up with the cry of the crow. The crow was crying out: "Everyone wake up! Meouraja has come to Iran! Meouraja, welcome to Iran!"Meouraja woke up, greeted him, and thanked him. The crow said: Pashul's friends are all crows' friends too. Meouraja entered the garden from inside the tree house; he was doing his morning exercise, when he saw birds in the garden. He said: "Hello rooster, how beautiful are the hen and chicks ... Hi, beautiful duck, dry yourself after swimming and be careful not to get cold... Hello sparrows ... The duck told the birds: "This is Meouraja that Pashul told us about, and the crows welcomed him. They were surprised and asked: "How do you know that? The duck said: "From his pearl necklace."

Then Meouraja talked about his morning program: "When I wake up, I do my exercise first, and then I wash my face, and wear my special Indian fragrance, which is a sign of an aristocratic cat with an ostrich aroma. This fragrance is very fragrant and makes me friend with all the birds. Meouraja was telling the birds about his running, that he had defeated the Bengal tiger. He said to the crow, which was sitting on the tree branch: "You count! See how many times I run around the garden." Then Meouraja ran around the garden five times.

The birds told him how fast he was, and he was really an athlete and could attend the Olympic Games. Then Meouraja went to wash his face, and wear his fragrance. Then he went to the birds and all the birds said: "How pleasant you smell! Meouraja, we are all your friends."Meouraja said, "I am your friend too."

At this time, Arezoo and Arman said good morning to each other. Arezoo said to Arman: "Pour some grain for the hens, roosters, ducks and the sparrows, some walnuts for the crows, and milk for Meouraja and Pashul to have breakfast. After having their breakfast, Pashul asked Arezoo: "May I show the city of Isfahan, AliQapu and The Bridge of thirty-three to Meouraja today?" "Of course you can, just watch the cars and bikes as you cross the streets." Then Pashul and Meouraja started off. Pashul said to Meouraja that it was not too far from Arezoo's house to the bridge of thirty-three; also the bridge and AliQapu are slightly spaced apart.

What a beautiful bridge! The snow was gradually melting; under the bridge a beautiful river was running. This historic bridge dates back to 400 years ago, and is one of the world's architectural masterpieces.

Meouraja told Pashul, "I asked your address from the cats on the bridge last night." Pashul said, "Let's go to Ali Qapu, where the chariots with beautiful horses round the whole garden. There, tourists enjoy riding in the carriage to see the beautiful landscape."Meouraja said to Pashul: "What a beautiful mansion!, How beautiful the horses and carriages are! Ramaraja had already told about the beauties of Isfahan." Pashul said she would ask Arezoo to show them MenarJonban (the shaking minarets) too and take them to the garden of birds with her. At that time, a sparrow fell from the tree on the ground; its nest was on the tree. Pashul said to the sparrow, "Do not be scared of us. I am Pashul and this is my friend Meouraja who came here from India. Right now, I make you warm in my fur and take you to your nest on the tree. We are your friend." Then she said, "If you like come to Arezoo's garden. All the crows know the address, and show you the way." The sparrow thanked Pashul for her kindness. Then Pashul who was coming down fell from the frozen tree to the ground. Meouraja shouted Help! Help! At this time, two girls approached them and helped Pashul. "Our house is near here," Meouraja said. "Please help to take her home." Meouraja was worried and repeatedly asked, "Is she fine?" One of them replied to Meouraja, "Yes, Pashul is a beautiful cat, she has just gone dizzy."Meouraja explained to them that Pashul went up to the tree to help the sparrow to take it to its nest, but suddenly fell from the top of the tree. Then they walked together towards Arezoo' shouse.

The names of those two girls were Sedigheh and Sara. They arrived at the house and rang the bell. Arezoo opened the door and welcomed them, Sedigheh said to Arezoo: "We work at the Children's Cancer Institute and we are raising fund for the institute. We were on our mission that we saw the sad incident of Pashul falling from the top on the tree, and we brought her here to you." Arezoo asked: "How is my cat?" Then she thanked them and invited them into the house and brought them some tea to make them warm. Meouraja wanted to help the institute so much, so he said: "I don't have any money, but I have a pearl necklace from the Indian Ocean that Nila has given it to me. I donate this necklace to your institute, this is my only asset. Please accept it from me."Sedigheh thanked Meouraja and accepted his gift. Then she asked about Pashul's health from Arezoo: Arezoo replied: "Pashul is good. Her hands and legs are OK. She must get some rest. I will put her in her tree house, so that she gets better soon." The crow cried out in the garden and around, Pashul fell off a tree on the ground when helping a sparrow. Pashul is a hero.

Meouraja said; "Rooster and crow, please do not sing tomorrow morning, so that Pashul can relax and can get better soon. Meouraja shall thank you all."

"Hello Ms. Fereshteh.""Hello Sedigheh and Sara.""How was the donation today?""Good, as usual people helped well, and today a cat helped our institute, he gave us a pearl necklace of original and precious value!" "May I see the necklace? Wow! What a beautiful necklace, and how big the pearls are! ... This necklace should be original. Are you sure a cat gave you this necklace?""Yes, it was a doctor's cat, they lived in a large dream mansion with a large garden, and they were rich" ... "Tomorrow, we will go to see Dr. Arezoo and the cat. I will take this necklace to the jewelry market."

The next morning, Pashul woke up and said: "Good morning, beautiful Arezoo."

And Arezoo said good morning to Pashul. Arezoo said, "Meouraja, today nothing is heard of the crows? The rooster does not sing?"Meouraja said, "I told them Pashul should rest to be good soon, therefore I asked them not to sing today."

A few hours later the bell rang, and Sedigheh, Sarah and Fereshteh came to the garden, Sedigheh said; "Ms. Fereshteh come with us to see Meouraja from near and get acquainted with Dr Arezoo.""I have come to see a cat who gave a necklace to Sedigheh and Sarah to help the institute."At this time, Meouraja came in and greeted everyone, and welcomed the guests. Fereshteh said: "Yesterday, he donated a pearl necklace worth 5 million toman to the Children's Cancer Institute, and I wanted to know if he regretted that." Meouraja said, "The value of your help and institute to children is much more than the value of my necklace."

Dr. Arezoo said: "I am very grateful to you and Meouraja. Meouraja taught me a great lesson. From today on, I will treat all the patients who are poor free of charge. Today, I will have some notices printed to be hung everywhere in Isfahan on the walls that reads: "Free Treatment of the Poor."Fereshteh saw a little mouse and screamed ...Arezoo said:"Do not be scared of them, they are my friends who came to help me if I need them, because of the magical necklace of the Temple of Karni Mata, which I tell you about later."Arezoo then contacted the printing house and told them to send her a thousand copies of this notice: "Visiting all the Poor in the Dr. Arezoo's Office is Free." To take part in this charity work, the print office did not charge Arezoo for printing these notices, and said he would send them in one hour to her house. Then Fereshteh said to Meouraja: "What a generous cat you are!, let me tap you, why are you greasy?" What a pleasant scent! Meouraja also replied, "I rub the oil of the sea whales so that my skin is softened and I wear the ostrich fragrance on myself so that all the birds will love me, because it is a sign of peace and friendship. Fereshteh said: "Tomorrow, Sedigheh and Sarah will help you stick the notices."Everyone said goodbye to of Dr. Arezoo, Pashul, and Meouraja to sell the necklace and raise money for the children's cancer institute.

Pashul thanked Meouraja for donating his precious and beautiful necklace, and Meouraja replied, "If I had the world, I would give it for you."

The mouse was staring at the sky and said, "What a beautiful night!" Hi Arezoo, May I ask you why are you alone? Where is your husband? "My husband left me and Arman many years ago and went to the United States forever," said Arezoo. The mouse replied: "Do not be upset. He didn't appreciate you and your ideals, you are a beautiful kind woman and you welcome all birds and animals in the garden of your house. Everyone loves you, the better he went. A painter lives in a villa facing you, his name is Mani, and he plays the guitar."Arezoo said, "I have heard of him. He is a very good guitar player." The little mouse said, "I will give him your message of peace and friendship. Good night Arezoo" ... After this conversation, everyone fell asleep.

The next morning was delightful and Meouraja woke Pashul up and told her: "We have a lot of work to do today and we have to help Sedigheh, Sarah and Arezoo to stick the notices." Arezoo woke up Arman and asked him to give breakfast to the birds and cats and then brush his teeth.

"Hello, nice and beautiful Arezoo.""Hi, my crow and my sweetheart messenger of good news.""What are you doing?" I want to stick the notes. "What did you write in the note?" I wrote I treat all the poor free of charge. "What a good thing. You are a kind and beautiful doctor. You are like angels. I also help you, now I tell all my friends to come and take the notes to their beak and fly to the sky and throw them down, but you have to give us walnut for that.""I accept, and I give you walnut as much as you like. There are always walnuts for you.""My friends and I make 55 crows. We come to your help."

A few days later, a beautiful voice from a neighboring house was heard. Pashul and Meouraja climbed up the wall to see what it was. They were two canaries, Pashul went by the cage of the canaries and greeted them, and then she introduced herself and Meouraja to them. But the canaries were very upset because they were in prison day and night. They wanted to be free and fly like every other bird. Meouraja tried to release them, but the cage was so tight that he couldn't.

Pashul said: "Meouraja came from India."The canaries asked, "Where is India?"She replied, it takes 20 days on the ocean by ship to come here from India. Canaries asked, "What are the ships and the ocean?"Meouraja answered, "The ship moves on the ocean. The ocean is much larger than the pool in your house, with whales, dolphins, sharks and beautiful fish."The canary said: "My wife and I have never seen a place other than this cage and this house." Pashul said: "I ask Arezoo to speak to the neighbor to release these canaries to come to her garden." The canaries said: "Tell Arezoo that there are two canaries in the cage and cannot fly, free us and let us fly like other birds."

Then Pashul and Meouraja went to Arezoo and told her that in the neighboring house, there are two canaries inside a cage; and if she would ask the neighbor to release them. Arezoo replied, "I ask the neighbor, but I do not think he releases them, because they are very expensive."Pashul insisted again: "I urge you Arezoo to ask your neighbor, because Meouraja and I have promised the canaries. Arezoo, you are rich and you can buy them."

Arezoo rang the bell in the neighbor's house. He opened the door to the villa for Arezoo and greeted her then he said: "Today I saw your notices in the city. You are a kind and respectable doctor."Arezoo, kindly asked the neighbor, "Would you sell your canaries to me?" The neighbor replied: "I will give them to you as a gift for your humanitarian action in the treatment of the poor."The cats were so happy to hear that. "Won't the cats eat the canaries?"The neighbor asked. She said, "No, the cats are very kind. They suggested that I buy them, so that I free them."Then the neighbor said, "I bring you the canaries now."Arezoo became very happy when she saw the canaries and said: "I am Arezoo, and I would like to take you to my garden and make a beautiful nest on top of Pashul and Meouraja home for you. The canaries said let's kiss you, Arezoo!

The canaries said, "Pashul and Meouraja are our friends, they had promised to free us and they did it." Days and weeks passed, and the winter was replaced by the spring. Arezoo had made a nest for the canaries on top of Pashul and Meouraja house on the tree. Arezoo treated more and more of the poor patients in her office for free, so there were fewer patients in the city than before, and five pharmacies in the city accepted to give free medicine to Dr. Arezoo's patients. Throughout the city, the patients prayed for the health and happiness of Arezoo and she became the most popular doctor of the city.

On one of these days, the little mouse went to visit Arezoo and told her that Mani and his mother are coming to her house with a box of sweets and a beautiful flower, so "Put on your beautiful dress and give yourself a savory fragrance."When the guests arrived, Mani's mother said: "Dr. Arezoo, People of Iran speak of your goodness in treating patients, and because of this, doctors from other cities are treating poor patients for free.

I have come to propose to you for Mani and I am sure that you are a good bride for me. Arezoo answered: "I must talk to my son about this matter." Arman, who was there, said to his mother: "I agree with this marriage. The rats, Meouraja and Pashul have already talked about it with me. Mani is a kind man."

20 Days Later

The news of Arezoo's wedding with Mani reached the Temple of Rats, Ramarjah and Nila. The King and Queen of Rats sent gifts of precious gold and jewelry for Arezoo. Ramaraja, Nila and Aditi decided to come from India to Iran and the beautiful city of Isfahan for the wedding ceremony. Arezoo was very happy when she heard this news. The canaries wanted to sing their best songs for the wedding ceremony, so that everyone would listen to their beautiful song and enjoy it. All the 55 crows were sleeping early to wake up early next morning. The next day, the crows delivered the news of Arezoo's wedding to the neighbors and fellow citizens of Arezoo, and said: "You are all invited to Arezoo's wedding; you are invited to have syrup, cream cake, walnuts and dinner."People of Isfahan prayed for Arezoo's prosperity.

Throughout the day, all friends and neighbors were busy setting tables and chairs, illuminating the garden, tying ribbons and preparing the garden for a wedding. The wedding ceremony began with joy, and the guests poured flowers on Arezoo.

Arezoo's beauty was unbelievable in the bridal gown. Ramaraja, Nila and Aditi were entertaining the garden with beautiful Indian jewels they had put on; all the guests rose up to the respect of their Indian guests and welcomed them. Nila presented Arezoo a jewel box, which was the gift of the King and Queen of Rats, Ramaraja shook hands with Mani, and Aditi became friend with Arman. Pashul and Meouraja went to Nila and threw himself in her arms. Fereshteh, Sedigheh, Sara and some others from the institute were also invited to the wedding.

Ramaraja congratulated Arezoo and Mani on their marriage and said, from young age, he has loved Iran, this ancient land and wished to come here and now he has this opportunity. He said, "I will travel again to Iran and Isfahan to trade, and I will also invite Iranian businessmen to come to India to trade."Then Ramaraja donated a portion of his wealth to the Children's Cancer Institute.

During the ceremony, Mani played the guitar for the guests and served them. The photographer took memory pictures from Arezoo, Mani and all the guests. Mani later drew a painting from this picture and hung it on the wall. The King of Rats sent a beautiful pearl necklace to Meouraja. A few days later Arezoo and Mani were drinking tea in the garden, while the canaries and sparrows were singing. Pashul and Meouraja were lying in a corner. Arman was playing in the garden. The neighbor was listening to the canaries in Arezoo's garden. They were singing more beautiful songs than the past, which was due to the magic of Arezoo's affection. Arezoo said to Mani: "I will wear Indian clothing at home from tomorrow, so that our Indian guests Meouraja doesn't feel like a stranger in this house." She also said to Mani: "I am the most prosperous woman in the world. Days passed, and it was the springtime when Mani, Arezoo, Arman, Pashul, and Meouraja went to the garden of birds, so Meouraja wore his own special ostrich fragrance. With Meouraja fragrance, which signed peace and friendship with the birds, and the knowledge of freeing the canaries by Arezoo, and Pashul and Meouraja helping the sparrow, had reached there too, so all the birds started singing which added to the beauty of the garden and was heard all over the city of Isfahan. Also the little mouse delivered the news of Arezoo's happiness and well-being to the King and Queen of Rats at Karni Mata Temple in India.

THE END